Dulcie's Taste of Magic

WRITTEN BY
GAIL HERMAN

ILLUSTRATED BY
JUDITH HOLMES CLARKE, ADRIENNE BROWN,
AND CHARLES PICKENS

HarperCollins *Children's Books*

First published in the USA by Disney Press,
114 Fifth Avenue, New York, New York, 10011-5690.

First published in Great Britain in 2007
by HarperCollins Children's Books.
HarperCollins Children's Books is a division of
HarperCollins Publishers,
77 - 85 Fulham Palace Road, Hammersmith, London, W6 8JB.

The HarperCollins Children's Books website is
www.harpercollinschildrensbooks.co.uk

978-0-00-722308-4
0-00-722308-0

1

Printed and bound in the UK

Visit disneyfairies.com

This book is proudly printed on paper which contains wood
from well managed forests, certified in accordance with
the rules of the Forest Stewardship Council.
For more information about FSC,
please visit www.fsc-uk.org

Mixed Sources
Product group from well-managed
forests and other controlled sources
www.fsc.org Cert no. SW-COC-1806
© 1996 Forest Stewardship Council

Dulcie's Taste of Magic

Jemma

All About Fairies

IF YOU HEAD toward the second star on your right and fly straight on till morning, you'll come to Never Land, a magical island where mermaids play and children never grow up.

When you arrive, you might hear something like the tinkling of little bells. Follow that sound and you'll find Pixie Hollow, the secret heart of Never Land.

A great old maple tree grows in Pixie

Hollow, and in it live hundreds of fairies and sparrow men. Some of them can do water magic, others can fly like the wind, and still others can speak to animals. You see, Pixie Hollow is the Never fairies' kingdom, and each fairy who lives there has a special, extraordinary talent.

Not far from the Home Tree, nestled in the branches of a hawthorn, is Mother Dove, the most magical creature of all. She sits on her egg, watching over the fairies, who in turn watch over her. For as long as Mother Dove's egg stays well and whole, no one in Never Land will ever grow old.

Once, Mother Dove's egg *was* broken. But we are not telling the story of the egg here. Now it is time for Dulcies's tale...

Dulcie's
Taste
of
Magic

DULCIE FIXED HER baker's hat. She smoothed her leaf apron. She flew through the Home Tree tearoom.

She did everything at the same time, and all in a panic.

"I can't believe I slept late," she muttered.

The sun was rising. She should already have been working. She should have been sorting ingredients for breakfast and giving orders. But here she was, just stumbling through the kitchen door.

Dulcie was a baking-talent fairy. Every fairy and sparrow man agreed that she was an incredible baker. She made the most perfect cupcakes, rolls, cookies, and muffins in Pixie Hollow. She baked three meals a day, seven days a week. And she never got tired. Well… never until lately.

On the other side of the swinging door, Dulcie stopped short. The kitchen was in chaos.

Confused shouts rang through the room. Baking talents scurried here and there. They flung open cabinets. They slammed them shut.

They lined up bowls and spoons. They shuffled them around.

They bumped into cooking-talent fairies who were scrambling eggs. They skittered into tea-serving fairies who were pouring tea.

Nothing was getting done.

"What should we do now?" cried

Dunkin, a baking-talent sparrow man. "We need Dulcie!"

Dulcie opened her mouth to speak. But suddenly a loud voice announced, "Nonsense! We'll be fine without her."

It was Ginger. Dulcie didn't know this baking-talent fairy very well. Ginger had arrived in Pixie Hollow just a short while before.

Ginger rubbed her hands together, eager to spring into action. "Now," she began, "here's what – "

"Dulcie!" Dunkin called out when he saw her. "You're here!"

He darted over to Dulcie, followed by the other baking talents. They crowded around, grinning.

"Thank goodness!" said Mixie, one of the baking talents. "Quick!

Tell us what to do."

Dulcie glanced into the tearoom. Already, fairies were sitting at the tables.

"We've got to move quickly," she said. "Mixie, get the milk pitchers and flour sacks. Dunkin, grab the biggest mixing bowl you can find. We'll bake one huge batch of blueberry muffins."

Dulcie began to get the batter ready, still giving orders. She whirled to face an egg-collecting fairy. "Put those eggs there!" she commanded.

"No, no!" she shouted to a harvesting fairy. "We need a different blueberry. A bigger one!"

She tapped her foot, waiting.

What a terrible start to the morning. First she was late. Now she didn't have the right ingredients!

Finally, she said, "Forget the blueberries. Forget the muffins. I'll bake my poppy puff rolls!"

Poppy puff rolls were Dulcie's speciality. Everyone loved them. Mixie and Dunkin sighed with relief.

Dulcie pushed aside the bowls. "We'll have to start over."

"You'd better speed it up." Ginger stood off to the side. She wasn't doing anything to help, Dulcie noticed.

Ginger pointed to the tearoom. It was filling up fast. "There's not much time, Dulcie. And those fairies look hungry!"

Dulcie tried to ignore her. She needed to think. But Ginger wouldn't stop talking.

"Oops! Be careful not to spill, Dulcie. Hurry, Dulcie! You need to stir faster. Remember, Dulcie, breakfast doesn't last all day."

Seconds ticked by. Dulcie mixed the dough. She poured in the poppy seeds. But she felt more and more rattled.

"Uh-oh. Queen Clarion is in the tearoom," Ginger reported from a spot near the door. "She's spreading her napkin across her lap. Now she's picking up her fork and knife. She's looking at the kitchen."

"Don't listen. Don't listen," Dulcie told herself.

She patted the dough into roll shapes. "Oh, no!" Her elbow knocked a ladle to the floor. Mixie quickly gave her a clean one.

"Fifteen. Twenty. Thirty." Dulcie counted the rolls. Her heart sank. There weren't enough. She needed more dough. "Get me more flour!" she barked.

Nobody was moving fast enough. So Dulcie grabbed a nearby sack. She poured the flour into the batter and tossed away the bag.

Meanwhile, serving-talent fairies flew into and out of the kitchen.

"Eggs coming up! First egg, sunny-side up," Dinah, a cooking-talent fairy, declared.

Dulcie groaned. One egg was done. Tea had already been served. She was really behind. She'd never been late before!

"Second egg ready," announced Dinah. "Egg à la Never Land."

A serving-talent sparrow man flew up next to Dulcie. "Are the rolls ready yet?" he asked.

"Almost!" Shaking a bit, Dulcie shaped the extra dough. Then she sprinkled fairy dust on the rolls, to make them bake faster. "Just a little longer!" She pushed the tray into the oven.

Ginger smirked. "A little longer?" she repeated. "Looks like those poppy puffs will have to be served with lunch."

"Really, one more minute," Dulcie promised the sparrow man. "Then everything will be ready."

Dulcie's stomach flipped like a pancake on a griddle. "At least, I hope it will be," she added to herself. She peeked out the kitchen door.

In the tearoom, fairies sipped tea and ate the eggs. A few glanced at her curiously.

Tinker Bell flew over to see what was the matter. "Are you having a problem, Dulcie? Anything wrong with those baking trays I fixed?"

"No." Dulcie shook her head. "Don't worry, everyone," she said in a loud voice. She tried to sound cheerful. "Poppy puff rolls for every table, coming right up!"

Dulcie rushed back to the oven. *The rolls must be done by now,* she thought. She pulled out the tray.

"Oh!" she gasped.

The rolls were flat.

"I thought you were making poppy puff *rolls*," Ginger said in an amused voice. "Not poppy pancakes."

"Why didn't they rise?" Dulcie moaned. Hesitantly, she took a bite.

"Ugh!" She made a face. "That's awful!"

Ginger picked up a crumpled sack from the floor. "Maybe because you used this instead of flour."

Dulcie grabbed the bag. There, as plain as day, was one word: *SALT*. Salt instead of flour? How could she have made such a mistake?

More frantic than ever, Dulcie flew in circles. "Hurry, Mixie! Dunkin!" she ordered. "We need to make another batch." She reached for a new sack of flour.

No one else moved. "Come on," she urged. "Why isn't anyone helping?"

"Because it's too late," a gentle voice said. Dulcie looked up. Queen Clarion stood by the door. "Breakfast is over."

Dulcie sighed. All that scrambling for nothing.

"All right," she said to the baking talents. "Let's have the cleaning fairies tidy up a bit. Then we can get those rolls ready for lunch."

There will have to be plenty of poppy puffs, she thought. *And they'll have to be especially good.* She had to make up for breakfast.

Dulcie opened the new bag of flour.

"Wait a minute, Dulcie." Queen Clarion placed her hand on Dulcie's arm. "Slow down."

"Slow down?" Dulcie squeaked. Why, anyone who knew her knew she *never* slowed down. She was always working, always busy.

"Yes." Queen Clarion nodded. "Slow down. In fact, you should take a real rest. You've been working nonstop ever since I can remember. Don't you think you deserve a holiday?"

Dulcie gazed at her, unable to speak. All this because she hadn't got the rolls out in time? Because she had made one little mistake confusing salt with flour?

"But, but... ," Dulcie sputtered. She couldn't stop baking. She just couldn't. She barely ever left the Home Tree kitchen. She was too busy baking. And that was how she liked it.

But Queen Clarion had made a decision.

"Who will take care of the kitchen?" Dulcie asked.

She turned toward the other baking talents. Dunkin and Mixie stared at their feet. No one would meet her gaze.

Only Ginger looked Dulcie in the eye. She stepped forward. "I'll take over," she said. "In fact, I'll start right now. Let's get lots of biscuits ready." She paused, then added, "There wasn't much to eat at breakfast."

Dulcie's wings twitched at the mention of biscuits. She itched to get baking. But Queen Clarion gently steered her out of the way.

"It will be fine," Queen Clarion assured her. "A few days off and you'll feel like a new fairy."

"Well," Dulcie said slowly, "I guess I'll just go, then."

Her wings dragging, she left the kitchen. She trudged through the tearoom, not even bothering to fly.

Too late, Dulcie realised she was

hungry. The delicious smell of biscuits already drifted through the air. But she wasn't going back. No way would she eat Ginger's biscuits!

2

BACK AND FORTH. Back and forth. Dulcie paced in her room in the Home Tree.

That annoying Ginger! Imagine, her taking over the kitchen. *I didn't arrive yesterday*, Dulcie thought. She knew that Ginger wasn't trying to be helpful or lending a wing to a friend in need. Ginger was showing off. She wanted everyone to know that *she* should be in charge.

Dulcie kept pacing. Back and forth. Back and forth.

Finally, she sat on the edge of her bed. She tapped her foot. She swung her leg. After a few seconds, she jumped up and started pacing again.

"Face it," she said to herself. "You can't sit still."

If she couldn't work, if she was forced to take a break, well, then she'd plan every minute. She wouldn't let herself just think about Ginger.

Dulcie took a deep breath. So what should she do? Pixie Hollow was big. There were plenty of spots she could visit. She could go anywhere and do anything. Why, fairies such as Tinker Bell and Vidia, a fast-flying-talent fairy, had even travelled outside Pixie Hollow, exploring different places in Never Land. Of course, Dulcie wouldn't do that. The very idea of leaving Pixie Hollow was scary. But there were many sights close by. And she had so much time!

She flew out her door, determined to keep busy. First she'd go to Havendish Stream. She'd dip her feet in the cool, clear water. That would be fun.

Let's see, Dulcie thought as she flew outside. *Which part of Havendish Stream should I visit?*

The stream ran all through Pixie Hollow. But Dulcie wanted to choose the prettiest part. *Next to the orchard,* she decided. She hadn't been there in a long time. Still, she remembered a large cherry tree hanging over the water. *It will give me some nice shade,* she thought. Her stomach grumbled loudly. *And maybe a cherry for breakfast!*

It was odd not to be in the kitchen,

working. She never left the Home Tree in midmorning. Pixie Hollow seemed somehow different at that time. Honestly, she wasn't even certain which way to go.

She felt a little strange, as if she didn't quite belong.

Dulcie shrugged off the feeling and kept flying. She crossed Havendish Stream, once, twice, three times, trying to find the cherry tree.

Finally, she spied it ahead. "It's about time!" she said to herself. "I was all turned around!"

Even before she landed, Dulcie heard laughter. A group of water-talent fairies stood knee-deep in the stream.

"Hey!" Dulcie called out. She settled on the bank to watch.

"There's more over here," Rani said

to the other water fairies. She didn't notice Dulcie. "Silvermist! Humidia! Come help!"

Dulcie watched the fairies move to a murky patch of water. They plunged their hands into the stream. As they waved their fingers, the water around them magically cleared.

"What are you doing?" Dulcie called more loudly. Maybe they could sit down with her and share a cherry or two. She really was hungry.

This time Rani heard her. "We're cleaning the stream," she explained. "A band of raccoons walked through here last night and part of the bank collapsed. The animal talents told us the minnows were having trouble swimming. So we're clearing all the silt from the water."

"I'm busy, too!" Dulcie said. "I still have to visit Lily, get my wings washed, eat lunch… " Her voice trailed off. The fairies had already gone back to work. They hadn't heard a word she'd said.

And why should they stop to listen? They had an important job to do.

Not like Dulcie.

"Well, I must be off," Dulcie said. And not staying to dip her toes, or even to pick a cherry, she flew away.

Dulcie flew east, southeast, west, southwest. She was searching for Lily's garden.

"This is ridiculous," she said, fuming. "I should know exactly where it is." But when she stopped to think, she couldn't remember the last time she'd been there.

Finally, Dulcie spotted the garden, just a couple of frog's leaps from the Home Tree. Inside, she took a deep breath. The flowers smelled sweet. Everything looked pretty. She could relax at last.

Really, I feel sorry for those water fairies, she thought. *They're working so hard. They're not on vacation like me.*

Dulcie stretched. Now she and Lily could have a nice talk. They'd sit under a lilac and watch the clouds roll past.

"Lily?" she called. "Are you here?"

"I'm in this corner!" Lily answered. "By the raspberry bush."

Dulcie hurried over. Lily was

kneeling on the ground. She sifted dirt through her fingers.

Good, Dulcie thought. *Lily isn't doing much of anything. She'll have plenty of time to spend with me.*

Dulcie plopped down next to her.

"Not there!" Lily cried.

Dulcie scrambled into the air. "What is it?" she asked. "Poison ivy?"

"A new flower is starting to grow. I'm spreading fresh soil to help it."

"Oh." Dulcie hovered above the ground. Was that all? "Why don't you take a break, Lily? We can sit and talk and catch up."

Dulcie's stomach rumbled loudly again. "And maybe you'd like to share a raspberry?" she added.

"Oh, I wish I could." Lily moved a

few inches and sprinkled more soil on the ground. "But I need to keep careful watch over this flower. It could sprout at any moment, and I want to be here. You know, to help it along."

Lily sat back on her heels. "Can you wait until I'm done?"

"Oh, I wish I could," Dulcie echoed Lily. "I need to... well, I need to get going," she finished in a hurry.

Why, oh why, did everyone have important work to do?

"Dulcie, wait!" Lily called.

But Dulcie had already gone, after stopping long enough to pick a raspberry.

Dulcie flew one way, then another. She didn't have a direction. She'd already visited two places, and not even an hour had passed!

Finally, she circled back to the Home Tree. She couldn't help it. She hated to be far from the kitchen.

"I'll just take a peek inside," Dulcie said to herself. "See how the fairies are doing without me." She pictured the scene from that morning: all the fairies racing around without a clue – until *she'd* arrived.

"They probably need my help. And when I fix everything, Queen Clarion will see that I should go back to work. Why, these few hours off have done wonders." Dulcie flapped her wings energetically. "I feel terrific!"

Dulcie flew through the Home Tree door. Dunkin and Mixie were pinching piecrust. A sparrow man slid a tray of buns into the oven. Other baking talents flitted around the kitchen, gathering ingredients, pouring batter, and –

Oh, no! Dulcie thought. *Smiling!*

Then she saw Ginger. Ginger was darting here and there, making sure everyone was doing his or her job.

All the fairies were so busy, no one noticed Dulcie. Ginger popped a steaming biscuit into her mouth. "Perfect!" she declared.

Dulcie had never felt so useless in her life. She took one last look around the kitchen. Then, quietly, she slipped out the door.

3

As Dulcie left the kitchen, fairies were flying to the tearoom for lunch. But Dulcie didn't want to be anywhere near Ginger… or her biscuits.

Slowly, she wandered through the Home Tree. Before long, she found herself outside the library.

"Hmmm," she said. "I never have enough time to read. But now… " She sighed. "Now I have all the time in the world." She tried to look on the bright side. "I can learn so much. About everything!"

Dulcie flitted to the history section. "'The History of Never Land,'" she read. She pulled the book from a shelf. "This sounds interesting."

She flew to another set of shelves. "Here's a gardening book. After I read this, I can share some ideas with Lily."

Next she took a book about fairy holidays, and one that told the legend of the first Never fairy. She stacked the books on a table without opening any.

When she glanced up, the cooking section was right in front of her. "Well," she said happily. "Here I am. Right where I belong." If she couldn't bake, at least she could read about baking.

She opened book after book. It felt good to see the recipes. She knew them all so well. Each one was like an old friend.

Suddenly, a piece of paper fluttered down from a high shelf, right past Dulcie's nose. She picked it up. It felt heavier than leaf paper. Its edges were curled, and it was yellow. It seemed ancient.

That's it! Dulcie realised. The paper was parchment, a material used by fairies long ago.

She blew off a layer of dust. Clearly, this piece of parchment hadn't been read by anyone in years. She studied it carefully.

"Why, it's written in Leaf Lettering!"

Long before, fairies didn't have the regular alphabet. They used leaf symbols instead of letters. It was such an old style of writing, fairies almost never used it anymore. And Dulcie's leaf-symbol reading was rusty.

She shook her head in frustration. Perhaps more light would help. She edged closer to the window and squinted at the symbols.

"That first one looks like a C," she

murmured. "Then O, then M." She translated letter by letter. Then she took a pencil and leaf paper and wrote out each one.

It spelled "Comforte Cayke."

"Comfort Cake?" Dulcie said out loud. "Why, I've never heard of it."

It must be an ancient recipe, she thought. Something very old but, at the same time, new and different to her. And maybe, just maybe, it had some ancient magic to it, too.

Dulcie's heart beat quickly. She was growing more and more excited.

"'An extraordinary cayke,'" she translated, "'that when baked will...'"

The rest of the sentence was rubbed off. The words were impossible to make out. There were no directions after it.

And as far as she could tell, just one ingredient was listed.

The recipe wasn't a recipe at all. Dulcie's heartbeat slowed. Her excitement faded.

If only she could make this cake… If only she could bring something to Never Land that had been missing for so long…

She sat on the floor to figure out the rest of the symbols. *THREE*, she wrote out carefully.

Three! The first word was "three."

Then came "sacks," then "flour." Three sacks flour!

Dulcie shook her head. The cake needed only flour? And plain, ordinary flour at that? That wasn't magical at all. There had to be more.

Dulcie turned the parchment this way and that. But there were no more clues.

Well, that was that. She was supposed to be relaxing, anyway. She shouldn't be thinking about baking so much as a cookie, much less an ancient cake.

But Dulcie couldn't put the parchment back on the shelf. She couldn't leave it behind. It didn't feel right.

She slipped the recipe between her books and left the library.

4

THE HOME TREE halls buzzed with activity. Fairies were leaving the tearoom. Dulcie stopped and sniffed. Delicious smells floated out the door.

"Dulcie," Lily said, flying over to her. "How was your morning?"

"I'm having a wonderful time!" Dulcie fibbed. She didn't want anyone feeling sorry for her.

She showed Lily her library books. "I'm planning to get lots of reading done. I couldn't be happier."

"Really?" Lily gave her a long look.

Dulcie sighed. "No, not really," she confessed. "I miss baking and my kitchen so much!"

Lily nodded. "It must be hard. Why,

if I couldn't work in my garden, I don't know what I'd do."

"And imagine what it would be like if someone else, like Iris, took your place!" Dulcie added.

Iris was another garden-talent fairy. She didn't have her own garden. But she knew a lot about flowers, plants, and trees. And she sure acted like it.

"Well," Dulcie went on, "that's how I feel about that tricky Ginger taking over the kitchen."

Hastily, Lily hid something behind her back.

Dulcie peeked around. "What's that?"

Just then, Iris flew over. "Oh, Lily!" she sang. "Is that an extra poppy puff roll you're holding? If you're not going to eat it, can I have it? The rolls are

33

delicious today. Remind me to tell Ginger how much I like them!"

Lily blushed. Slowly, she brought out the roll. "You can have it, Iris."

"Mmm!" Iris said.

Dulcie could barely speak. Her glow flared bright orange, she was so angry. But not at Lily. At Ginger.

Ginger was baking Dulcie's speciality! Her most famous treat! It wasn't fair. It wasn't right. Dulcie had to show Ginger she was still in charge.

Dulcie flew to her room. She dropped the books on her bed.

She *was* going to do something. Definitely. But what?

Once again, the ancient recipe caught

Dulcie's eye.

What if the cake was so delicious… so tasty… so amazing… that all the fairies begged for Dulcie to come back to the kitchen? Then no one would think Ginger should be in charge – ever again.

It didn't seem to be a real recipe. But still…

"One step at a time," Dulcie told herself. First she'd get the flour. She grabbed the parchment and flew out the door, headed for the fairy-dust mill.

Dulcie had never thought much about how ingredients got to her kitchen. She'd been too busy. But now, she would have to find flour on her own. The cake had to be a surprise. After all, Dulcie was on vacation. She wasn't supposed to be baking.

She needed to be sneaky. And fast. One more day of Ginger being in charge, and no one would remember Dulcie. She'd be as stale as two-day-old bread.

Dulcie flew quickly, but not too quickly. She didn't want to look like she was in a hurry. That might make the other fairies wonder.

"Just taking a flight around Pixie Hollow," she called out each time she saw another fairy. "Not doing much."

At last, Dulcie reached the mill. She slipped quietly inside. Then she darted behind a bin and peeked out.

Fairies and sparrow men fluttered busily about. In one section of the mill, fairies measured out fairy dust.

Two harvest-talent fairies, named

Pell and Pluck, worked in another section. They were placing stalks of wheat in piles. As they walked, the tufts on the ends of the wheat brushed their noses.

"Achoo!" Pluck sneezed.

"Here," said Pell. She handed Pluck a leafkerchief.

Then Pell sneezed, and Pluck gave Pell *her* leafkerchief.

The two made trip after trip. Each stalk was three times the size of a fairy, and hard to balance. Pluck and Pell teetered and tottered. They sneezed and blew their noses. But they didn't stop.

Meanwhile, other fairies separated the seeds from the stalks. A third group carried the seeds up to a hollowed-out log that was cut in half to form a chute. They dropped the seeds inside.

The seeds rolled down the chute and fell through a funnel. At the bottom, the millstone ground the seeds into flour.

A waiting fairy scooped up the flour and put it into sacks. Then a fairy named Maisy hefted it onto her shoulder and flew away.

Dulcie watched with growing interest. *Why, this is fascinating,* she thought.

She'd had no idea that making flour took such skill and hard work. But she didn't have time to think about that now. She needed to spring into action.

It shouldn't be difficult to take some flour. Surely no one would notice if she borrowed one or two or three sacks.

She would take the sack just after it was filled but before Maisy returned.

Dulcie slid behind a seed bin. She

waited… There! The fairy had filled the sack with flour and set it aside.

For a moment, no one was around.

Dulcie wrapped her arms around the sack of flour. She hugged it and tried to rise into the air. But the bag was heavy! Dulcie fell over, knocking the bag to the ground. Flour spilled everywhere.

She hid behind the bin.

"Oh!" Maisy came back. She shook her head as she spotted the spilled flour. With a sigh, she swept it up. Then she hoisted the sack onto her shoulder and flew off.

Dulcie was ready for the next sack. She sprinkled a bit of fairy dust onto it. "Whew!" She could lift it right up.

Suddenly, Maisy landed beside her. "I'll take it from here, Dulcie. Remember, no work for you. You're resting!"

Dulcie smiled brightly. "You're right, of course, Maisy. Guess I'll be off, then!"

Dulcie flew out of the mill. She needed a new plan.

Why not just follow Maisy and see where she stores the flour? she decided.

She trailed Maisy away from the mill, around hedges and bushes, past plants and flowers, to the Home Tree, and straight into the kitchen pantry!

Dulcie peeped through a window. She saw Maisy put the sack on a pantry shelf. That was it! Dulcie realised. The flour went right to the kitchen!

She waited for Maisy to leave. Then, quickly, she moved the flour to a corner behind the acorn bins. There! She wiped her hands on her apron. The flour was completely hidden.

"Now," she said to herself, "I'll just wait here for Maisy to come back with more!"

A little while later, Maisy returned with another sack. "How strange!" Maisy muttered. "Where is that other sack of flour?"

She looked around, never thinking to check the corner.

She shrugged. "I'll just have to get more."

The same thing happened again and again. Each time, Dulcie hid the sack. Each time, Maisy scratched her head, confused.

Finally, Maisy flew into the kitchen and spotted Ginger. "Aha!" she said. "*You've* been using the new flour!"

Ginger snapped, "What new flour? I've only been here two minutes. And I don't have any flour! Where is it?"

"All right, all right." Maisy drew herself up. "You don't have to get huffy about it."

For a second, Dulcie felt bad. But she couldn't worry about Ginger's temper. She sneaked upstairs to her room.

Dulcie picked up the ancient recipe. If only there were more to it!

"I've got the flour," she whispered. "Now what?"

One by one, leaf symbols appeared on the parchment. Dulcie grinned. She had been right! This *was* a magical recipe.

She had proved she could get the

flour. She had performed a task. And something had happened! More writing!

Slowly, she translated the symbols: *one egg.*

How would she manage that?

5

DULCIE HOVERED outside the Home Tree. She was trying to figure out which way to go.

"Eggs, eggs, eggs," she muttered to herself.

Fresh eggs were delivered to her kitchen every morning. Dulcie just used them. She didn't know anything about getting them.

Where did egg-collecting fairies go? She felt a little embarrassed admitting it, but she had no idea.

I have to find an egg collector, Dulcie thought, *and follow her, just like I did Maisy.*

She hurried to the Home Tree lobby. She sat down on a toadstool chair and pretended to relax.

One by one, fairies and sparrow men fluttered past. Half an hour went by before Dulcie spied Colette, an egg-collecting-talent fairy. She was carrying a cushioned basket half her size.

"She's collecting eggs! Right now!" Dulcie said.

Dulcie trailed Colette. Every time Colette stopped, Dulcie ducked behind a leaf. Every time Colette flew, so did Dulcie.

Finally, Colette came to the dairy barn, where the dairy mice lived. She flew a little beyond that to a grove of trees. Dulcie followed.

"I never knew these were here," Dulcie whispered. The trees were saplings, just four feet tall. They were covered with fluffy white blossoms and stood in a semicircle.

Robins twittered all around. Colette flew among them. She paused by a nest filled with eggs and put her ear close to one.

Even Dulcie knew that fairies used only empty eggs. They were eggs that wouldn't hatch. "She's listening for baby chicks!" Dulcie said to herself. Colette lifted a pale blue egg into her basket. Dulcie had used robins' eggs in lots of her recipes. They made delicious cakes and cookies.

Then Colette pulled a balloon carrier from behind a tall fern. She unwound the cord from the anchor root. Fairy dust-filled balloons lifted the carrier high off the ground.

Colette carefully pushed two more eggs into the balloon carrier. Pulling the carrier, she flew toward the Home Tree.

Dulcie now knew which nest had the empty eggs. But she wanted to check on the other ones. She flew to another tree and peered inside a nest.

Four blue eggs were nestled close together. Cracks lined each shell. *Tap, tap, tap.* The babies were breaking through. One by one, they poked their way out.

"Peep, peep!" They shook their wet feathers.

In a flash, the mama robin flew over.

Dulcie shook her head in wonder. Just think, all this had been happening right in Pixie Hollow. And she had never known!

Smiling and thinking of the tiny birds, Dulcie picked up an empty egg. She could barely get her arms all the way around it. She had to peek around the side of the egg as she flew. Once, she almost bumped into a blueberry bush. Then she saw a group of fairies flying nearby. She darted behind a leaf and waited for them to pass.

Before long, Dulcie poked her head into the kitchen. It was empty. Quickly, she hid the egg with the flour. Then she hurried to her room and took out the recipe. There, in bold symbols, was more writing: *five teacups sugar.*

Her next task! To get the sugar.

Dulcie thought for a long moment. Sugar came from sugarcane. And wasn't there a sugarcane field near Havendish Stream? She wasn't sure. But hadn't she seen a sign when she was circling that morning? Sweet Field. That could be it.

Away Dulcie flew. This time, she

didn't feel strange leaving the Home Tree. At least, not as strange.

Dulcie soon spied Sweet Field, which was full of sugarcane. Fairies and sparrow men flitted all around.

Dulcie ducked behind a big tree root. "I was right!" she said happily.

Some fairies, wielding axes, chopped at the sugarcane. Others pushed a big round stone over a fallen cane, squeezing out the sugary juice.

Two sparrow men boiled the juice in huge pots, turning it into a sticky brown mountain of sugar. Two more fairies shovelled the sugar into giant barrels. Then they rolled the barrels into the bottom of a hollow tree.

All I have to do is borrow one barrel, Dulcie thought. *That should be more than five teacups. Piece of cake!*

She waited for a fairy named Ava to leave the hollow tree. Then she sneaked inside. The place was filled with barrels!

But just then, another fairy brought in one more. The barrel rolled to a stop. It was so close to Dulcie that it pinned her wing against the tree wall.

She was stuck! She wriggled this way and that. But it didn't make a difference. She couldn't get free.

Dulcie groaned. She'd have to call for help. And she wouldn't be able to take a barrel. Not now. All the fairies would know. Instead, she scooped up handfuls of sugar and put them in her apron pockets.

"Hello?" she called out. "Anyone there?"

"Dulcie?" Ava flew over. "What are you doing here?"

"Oh, just taking in some sights. You know, I'm on vacation." She pointed at her wing. "Do you think you could help?" She hoped her pockets weren't bulging too much.

Ava moved the barrel. "Come back and visit anytime, Dulcie."

Dulcie smiled. Now that she knew exactly how to get to Sweet Field, maybe she would.

When Dulcie returned to her room, she checked the ancient recipe again. The next ingredient was waiting for her.

Four drops vanilla.

Dulcie loved vanilla. But she didn't

have a clue where it came from. Then she remembered the book she'd borrowed from the library, *The History of Never Land*.

She began to flip through the pages. Maybe there was something about long-ago fairies first finding vanilla.

She stopped at page 327. The entry read: *Fairies explore the vanilla orchids.*

Dulcie read on. Vanilla came from orchid plants. Now she knew what to do.

Vanilla. Chocolate. Nuts. Berries. One by one, the ingredients appeared on the parchment. And one by one, Dulcie found them with the help of her books.

With each trip, she grew a little bolder, a little more sure of herself.

By the time she found the almond orchard, Dulcie felt as if she'd visited every part of Pixie Hollow. And she'd seen so many different talents at work! She watched as the tree-picking talents used hacksaws to remove almond fruits from a tree. They wore helmets made of walnut shells to protect their heads. And their arms looked strong from carrying heavy nuts and fruit. Dulcie realised that many of the fairies did difficult – even dangerous – work. But they seemed to love it as much as she loved working in the kitchen.

After that trip, she sat on her bed to rest. Another ingredient had shown up. She translated each leaf symbol.

"Oh!" Dulcie caught her breath. The words read: *10 drops sweet syrup from the Creeping Treacle Vyne.*

6

THE CREEPING TREACLE VINE!

"I've never even heard of it," Dulcie said with a frown. She was sure this was the final ingredient. Once again, she would have to check *The History of Never Land.*

Dulcie spread open the big book. She looked over the contents page, then the index. No creeping treacle vine. Not one entry between "Captain Hook" and "cuddle vine."

Dulcie knew all about the cuddle vine. One grew in Lily's garden.

Lily! Maybe she could ask Lily about the creeping treacle vine.

Dulcie had wanted to do this all on her own. She wanted the cake to surprise everyone. But now she was so close. Lily would be such a help.

Maybe a vine was growing right in her garden.

Dulcie grabbed a pea-pod pack and took off for Lily's garden.

Seconds later, she flew over a raspberry hedge and landed in the soft grass.

"Dulcie!"

She stiffened. That voice! A little too loud. A little too shrill.

Iris rushed over to Dulcie. "I just heard why Ginger's been doing all the baking," she said.

Dulcie nodded glumly.

"That's how I lost my garden. I went away, and when I came back, it was gone."

Dulcie shook her head. She wouldn't let Iris make her feel worse. She wouldn't!

"Is Lily here?" she asked. "I have a question for her."

"No, but I can help."

"I don't know, Iris. This is a question about a certain plant."

"Well, I'm a garden fairy." Iris tossed her curly hair. "In fact, I know more than any other garden fairy around. So you can ask me anything."

Dulcie wanted to ask someone who tended an actual garden. Not Iris.

"Iris," she began. Then she stopped.

Dulcie was having a hard time being out of the kitchen for a day. Poor Iris had gone without a garden for much, much longer.

"Come on, Dulcie," Iris prodded. "You have a question. And I'll bet I have the answer right here in my book." She pulled out the plant book she carried with her everywhere.

Instead of working in a garden, Iris worked on her book. She'd been filling it with all sorts of information about the plants of Never Land.

Iris flipped open the birch-bark cover. "Is the question about poppy seeds? Or figs for pie? Pumpkins for cupcakes? Or maybe – "

"Wait!" Dulcie held up a hand. "Hold on, and I'll tell you!"

Iris blinked quickly. Was she going to cry?

"I just really need help," Dulcie said more gently. "Have you ever heard of the creeping treacle vine?"

Iris turned one page, then another, and another. "Weeeell" – she drew out the word – "of course I've heard of it. Every garden fairy has."

"You have?" Dulcie said. "So where is it?"

"I don't have proof that it's even real. It could just be a story told to every new garden talent."

Dulcie was confused. "What have you heard?"

Iris shrugged. "It's supposed to be very powerful. It holds some special magic. And you can find it in only one place in all of Never Land."

Iris paused. Dulcie leaned closer. "Tell me!" she squeaked. "Tell me."

"The Never Arbor," Iris whispered. "Deep in the forest, where no fairies go."

"Do you know where the Never Arbor is?"

Iris snapped her book shut. "Of course," she said in her regular voice. "I'm a garden fairy, aren't I?"

Dulcie nodded. Why wouldn't Iris just get to the point?

"It's on the southern tip of the forest. Start at the edge of Pixie Hollow, by that wild mint patch, and just keep going."

Iris made the trip sound simple. Dulcie could leave right then and still be back for dinner. "You've been helpful, Iris," she said. Right away, she headed for the mint patch.

But when she reached the sharp-smelling plants, she hesitated. The dense forest spread before her. To Dulcie it was a mysterious place, filled with mysterious creatures. She recalled Iris's whispered words: "The Never

Arbor, deep in the forest, where no fairies go."

The sun shone low in the sky. The day was almost over. There wasn't much time. If Dulcie didn't finish the cake today, Ginger would still be in charge tomorrow.

She took a deep breath. She hitched the pea-pod pack up on her shoulder.

"Dulcie?"

Dulcie jumped. Iris again?

Then she grinned. "Lily! What are you doing here?"

"Iris told me you were looking for me. What's going on?"

Dulcie hesitated. Should she tell Lily about the ancient recipe? Dulcie wasn't even good friends with Lily. But something made Dulcie want to trust her.

Dulcie took a deep breath and told her

about the recipe, about the ingredients that magically appeared, and finally about the sweet syrup from the creeping treacle vine.

She squeezed Lily's hands. "Come with me, Lily. Help me find the arbor!"

7

A DUSKY GLOW settled over the trees. Dulcie and Lily stood hand in hand at the edge of the forest.

"We fly around the dark woods," Lily told Dulcie. "Then we go through a prickly briar. From there, it should be a short trip to the Never Arbor."

Dulcie's heart thudded. They'd be going so far from Pixie Hollow! She felt nervous. Today she'd flown farther than she ever had before. But this journey would take her deep into no-fairy land, a place so far from the comforts of her kitchen, Dulcie couldn't even imagine it.

"We'd better go now," Lily said. She gazed at the sky. "While it's still light."

Dulcie straightened her wings. This

was it. The quest for the final ingredient. She slung the pea-pod pack over her shoulder. Then she and Lily took off through the trees.

It was darker and chillier in the woods.

Dulcie followed Lily deeper and deeper. She had to find this treacle vine. She had to prove she still had the magic touch in the kitchen.

The fairies flew farther. The trees grew close together here. Their leaves blocked the dimming sunlight.

"Oof!" Dulcie flew right into a pine tree branch. Thick, sticky ooze stuck to her wings. "What is it?" she cried.

Lily rushed over to wipe it off. "It's only sap. It's all right, Dulcie."

Dulcie shivered. "This place is spooky." Shadows danced around the leaves. Twisted branches seemed to jump into her path.

Dulcie started at a long, skinny shape in front of her.

"Watch out, Lily! There's a snake!" Dulcie shouted.

"It's just a stick," Lily said.

Dulcie was sure she saw a hawk overhead, then a fox on the ground. "Relax," Lily kept telling her. "You're imagining things."

The trees drew even closer together.

"We're in the briar now," Lily called out. "Be careful of thistles and burrs!"

"Ouch!" Something sharp poked Dulcie. "Ouch!" It happened again and again. She felt like a piecrust being pinched at the edges.

Meanwhile, Lily flew gracefully on.

She seemed to know where each plant and tree stood.

"Hang on, Dulcie," Lily called. "We're almost there."

Dulcie saw the red-gold sun setting behind the trees. She looked ahead. Was that a clearing in front of them?

Suddenly, something gripped her tightly. And this time, it wasn't Dulcie's imagination.

A long, thin leaf wrapped itself around her waist. She stared up at the towering plant. Bright blue petals formed a mouth. The flower bent hungrily toward her.

"Let me go!" she said. But the leaf gripped her more firmly.

Up, up. The leaf lifted her higher, toward the mouth. The petals opened wide.

Dulcie pounded on the leaf with her fists. But it just squeezed more tightly. It was squeezing her so hard, she couldn't call for help.

Dulcie gasped. She – who loved to bake more than anything – was going to be eaten!

"Don't move!" a voice whispered in her ear.

Lily hovered an inch away. "It's a snareweed plant. It must think you're a fly. But it only eats live bugs. If you don't move, it will let you go."

Dulcie took a small breath. She held her body still.

Nothing happened.

She stayed like that for ten seconds. Twenty seconds.

"You're doing great," Lily whispered.

A minute.

Finally, the leaf loosened. "Keep still!" Lily whispered again. "It has to let go completely."

A few more seconds passed. The leaf dropped away altogether.

Dulcie was free! Quickly, she flew out of the leaf's reach.

"Lily, you saved me!" she said. She hugged her friend.

Lily patted her back. "Those fly-eaters always scare the fairy dust off me! But look!" She pointed through the trees.

Dulcie spied an arch of bending boughs. It was the entrance to the clearing.

"It's the Never Arbor!" Lily exclaimed. She darted away, out of sight.

"Lily?" Dulcie called. She flew a few inches forward.

She waited a moment, listening. Then she called again. "Lily? Where are you?"

There was no answer.

"Lily! Lily!" Dulcie shouted. Had Lily flown too far to hear? Or had she been caught by another fly-eating plant?

"Lily!"

She strained to listen. Then she heard a faint voice. "Dulcie… "

"Lily?" Dulcie flew toward the sound, through the arch of bending branches.

"I'm over here!" The voice grew louder. "And I've found it! I've found the creeping treacle vine!"

8

DULCIE STOPPED short in the clearing. For a moment – just a moment – she didn't care about the creeping treacle vine. Or about the Comfort Cake, or even about Ginger. The Never Arbor pushed everything else out of her mind.

"It's amazing!" Dulcie whispered. Lily flew over to join her. Together, they gazed around.

Slender cypresses, grand cedars, and blossoming almond trees circled the open space.

Bluebells, marigolds, and other wildflowers grew by the dozens. Yellow, orange, and aquamarine petals covered the ground like a soft carpet. The setting sun cast a red glow over the flowers, plants, and trees.

Dulcie turned around slowly. She took in every view.

"It is beautiful," Lily agreed. "We must be the first fairies to see this place since... since... I don't know when."

Lily took Dulcie's hand. She led her through a sweet-smelling tangle of ferns. A boulder stood at the end. A long flowered vine wound around the rock. One end crept forward like an inchworm. The rest followed.

"This is it," said Lily. "The creeping treacle vine."

"You really did find it!" Dulcie said. She took a jug out of her pea-pod pack. "Now what?"

"We'll just take some syrup." Lily knelt next to the vine. She whispered something Dulcie couldn't hear. Then she gently lifted one end. Syrup dripped out.

Dulcie held out the jug to catch the treacle. Then, carefully, Lily put the vine back in place.

Dulcie grinned. "Let's go!"

The friends flew through the Never Arbor, back through the briar and the dark woods.

It's funny, Dulcie thought. *It seems much quicker going home. But maybe that's because I know the way.*

The places weren't as scary anymore. They were almost familiar. Dulcie even waved to the snareweed plant from a distance. It was only doing what it was supposed to do.

It was late by the time they got back to the Home Tree. Dulcie hugged Lily.

"You really helped me," she said.

"I'm glad I went." Lily smiled, then yawned. "Whew! I'm going right to sleep."

"Goodnight," Dulcie said. But *she* wasn't going to sleep. Now, in the dark of night, was the perfect time to start baking. No one would be in the kitchen.

Excited, she flew to her room. "I have the treacle!" she announced. She picked up the recipe. "Now what should I do?"

Leaf symbols slowly formed. Dulcie squinted. Was she translating this right? She expected to see "heat" and "stir" and "mix." Instead, she read only two words: "Goode Lucke."

That was it. Good luck.

Dulcie had no directions. No instructions. She'd have to rely on her own talents from here on. Alone in the kitchen, she washed her hands.

Then she pulled out baking pans. Big ones. Small ones. Round ones. Square ones. Star-shaped and heart-shaped pans that Tink had made especially for her.

Next she found the nutshell mixing bowls. Five different sizes, each one nesting inside the other. Then came whisks and spoons and knives and forks. "And finally," said Dulcie, "the ingredients!"

It was the middle of the night, but Dulcie felt wide awake. She poured and mixed. She stirred and blended. She sprinkled and drizzled.

Somehow, deep in her bones, Dulcie

knew just what to do. Which bowl to use for what. When to add each ingredient.

As she worked, she hummed to herself.

Hours passed. Dulcie kept baking, lost in her work.

Finally, she dripped two drops of treacle into each of the five mixing bowls. Then she poured all the batter into one giant pan. She wiped her hands on her leaf apron. There. It was done. She opened the oven.

But she hesitated. That deep-down feeling – that certainty of what to do – was gone.

The recipe was called Comfort Cake. And it used certain ingredients. But that was all Dulcie knew, really. What exactly had she made?

And how long should it stay in the oven?

"Oh, I hope I did everything right." Dulcie hefted the heavy pan and slid it inside.

The oven door closed with a quiet clank.

Dulcie sighed and gazed around the kitchen. The counters were piled high with dirty pans. The sink overflowed with unwashed bowls. Sugar and flour coated the floor.

"What a mess!" Dulcie whispered. She didn't have the strength to speak more loudly. All her energy drained away. She felt tired to the bone. She pulled out a chair and sat down. She'd rest, just for a moment, before cleaning up.

9

Sunlight streamed through the window. Voices whispered above Dulcie's head. "It looks like a tornado hit the kitchen." "Shhh! Dulcie's sleeping." "Should we wake her?" "What's going on?"

Then one loud voice rang out. "My kitchen! Something has to be done about this!"

Dulcie jumped to her feet, wide awake. It was Ginger who had spoken.

Everyone fell silent.

Dulcie gazed from face to face. First she looked at Ginger, whose cheeks blazed with anger. Then she turned to the worried-looking Dunkin and Mixie. Finally, she glanced at all the other

76

baking and cooking talents.

She felt so nervous, she couldn't speak. This was it. The cake had to be ready by now.

If she failed, would she ever be able to bake again?

"Well?" Ginger tapped her foot. "We're waiting for an explanation."

"Ahem." Dulcie cleared her throat. She told them about finding the ancient recipe. About gathering the ingredients. About staying up all night to bake. And finally, about wanting to create something no one had ever tasted before. As she talked, she could hear fairies coming into the tearoom.

Slam! The oven door banged open. Dulcie whirled around. Ginger was peeking inside.

Smiling, she turned to Dulcie. "Well," she said briskly, "let's serve Dulcie's surprise for breakfast. See what everyone thinks!"

Dulcie was amazed. Ginger wanted to serve the cake? Not keep it secret from all the fairies? Her heart soared. Maybe Ginger understood how Dulcie felt about baking. Maybe they could work together!

Or maybe…

Dulcie pulled out the pan. "Oh, no!" she cried.

The cake was flat. Just like the poppy puff rolls, it hadn't risen. Not one little bit.

In a flash, Ginger snatched the cake. She hurried through the kitchen doors. "Look, everyone!" she exclaimed.

"Dulcie's masterpiece!"

Dulcie rushed after Ginger. But it was too late. The tearoom was full of fairies. Queen Clarion, Tinker Bell, Lily – everyone stared at the cake.

One by one, the fairies edged closer. They sniffed. They craned their necks. They shook their heads.

"What is it?" Tinker Bell finally asked.

"I know! It's some kind of new-fangled bread," Iris said. "That's why it's flat."

"No, no," Queen Clarion said kindly. "Let's have Dulcie tell us."

Lily nodded. "Go ahead, Dulcie."

Dulcie held back a sob. "Well, it's supposed to be Comfort Cake."

"Comfort Cake?" Ginger said as Dulcie placed it on a table. "This can't be comfort food. Anyone who ate this would feel terrible!"

"I – I – I just wanted everyone to feel good," Dulcie stammered. "That's why I bake. To fill fairies with goodness."

And it was true, she realised. She didn't run the kitchen just to boss other fairies around. She didn't give orders just to make herself feel important. Well, at least she wouldn't anymore. No. The day before, she hadn't missed that part of her job at all. She had missed the baking. She had missed creating something for others to enjoy.

And, oh, how she wanted to go back to work!

10

"WELL, THAT'S IT, folks," Ginger said after a minute. "Now, if you'll excuse me, I have to get back to my kitchen. How do lemon popovers sound?"

"Yummy!" said Iris.

Everyone turned to go back to their seats. A few fairies patted Dulcie on the back.

Dulcie slumped. She'd go back to the kitchen, too. She'd help Ginger. She'd do whatever the other fairy said. No matter what, she had to keep baking. Even if it meant taking orders from Ginger.

"Wait, everyone!" Queen Clarion's voice rang through the room. "Look!"

Dulcie whirled around. All the fairies and sparrow men fluttered back.

Something was happening to the Comfort Cake. It trembled. It quivered and shook. Then, slowly, it began to grow.

"Stand back, everyone!" ordered Iris. "I've seen this happen with ivy. Give it room!"

The cake stretched wider and wider. It started to take shape.

"It's finding its form. Like metal becoming a pot or a pan," said Tinker Bell.

It was changing colour... shifting shades...

"It's like a rainbow," said Bess, an art-talent fairy.

The cake kept rising and rising. Then it gave a soft whoosh, like a sigh, and it stopped.

"Why," Lily gasped, "it's lovely!"

Dulcie couldn't believe her eyes.

The now giant Comfort Cake was composed of layer upon layer of sparkling cream and cake. Swirls and whorls of colourful icing, frosted flowers, and gleaming spun sugar decorated every part.

"Ooh!" the fairies said, almost at the same time.

Ginger sniffed. "It looks OK. But how does it taste?"

Serving talents rushed over. They had to fly nearly as high as the ceiling to reach the top. They cut big tasty-looking pieces, fluttering down as they worked, until they had reached the bottom and each slice of cake had been placed on a table.

Fairies and sparrow men scattered to their seats.

"It looks so good, I hate to eat it," Lily said.

"Oh, you must," Dulcie urged. She stepped forward and smiled. "That's what cake is for – to be enjoyed!"

Everyone lifted a fork. Dulcie closed her eyes. She couldn't look.

The Comfort Cake had to be delicious. It just had to be!

Lily scooped up a forkful of cake. "Strawberry. My favourite!"

"No, it isn't!" Tink called from the pots-and-pans-talent table. "It's chocolate cake. My favourite!"

"It's vanilla!" "It's cinnamon!" "No, no! Toasted almond!"

Fairies and sparrow men called out their cake flavours. Each one tasted his or her favourite kind.

Dulcie clapped her hands. She gazed around the room. Everyone was eating. Everyone was happy. Even Ginger was spooning up bites.

"Dulcie, it seems that your vacation is over," Queen Clarion said with a smile. "I should have known it wouldn't last long."

After breakfast, Dulcie flew through the Home Tree. She visited workshops, the laundry room, the storeroom.

Then she flew around Pixie Hollow. She stopped at the dairy barn, the mill, the fields, and the orchards.

Before her adventure, she'd never thought about other talents. She'd just ordered them around. Now she knew how hard each and every fairy worked.

"I'm grateful for all your hard work," she told Lympia in the laundry room.

"I know how tricky this is," she said to the egg-collecting fairies.

"And you harvesting fairies," she sighed with admiration, "you know so much."

It was fun flying from place to place. Every spot felt familiar. Not quite as familiar as the kitchen, but she was comfortable all over Pixie Hollow. She belonged everywhere!

Finally, Dulcie flew back to the kitchen. Cooking and baking fairies bustled about. Lunch preparation was just beginning.

For a moment, Dulcie just watched. It felt so good to be there!

"Oh!" Mixie saw Dulcie. "Every-one! Dulcie's here!"

In seconds, baking talents crowded around.

"What should we do for lunch, Dulcie?" asked Dunkin.

"Should we bake banana bread? Puff pastries?" Mixie asked.

Dulcie glanced around. Ginger stood off to the side, stirring a bowl with jerky, angry strokes. She glared at Dulcie.

Dulcie yawned. "Uh-oh," she told herself. "I really am tired."

She pictured her cozy room, her soft-as-a-marshmallow pillow. It seemed so inviting! She'd been up all hours of the night. Truthfully, she could use a break.

A little vacation.

She flitted over to Ginger's side. "Attention, baking talents!" Dulcie announced. "Ginger will be in charge of today's lunch."

Right away, Ginger set aside the bowl. She threw a look of victory at Dulcie. "So you finally figured out who should be boss," she said.

She opened her mouth wide, ready to take command.

"But," Dulcie interrupted, "I'll be back for dinner!"